I0703402

THE ADVENTURES OF CAPTAIN MIDNIGHT

AUTHOR

LAWANDA LEWIS BURRELL

CO-AUTHOR

NALIN CHASE BURRELL

SUSU Entertainment LLC
P.O. Box 1621
Cypress, TX 77410
www.sosweetauthor.com
susuentertainmentllc@gmail.com

Printed in the United States of America

Library of Congress Cataloging-in-Publication Data

Names: LaWanda Lewis Burrell, Author | Nalin Chase Burrell, Co-Author

Title: The Adventures of Captain Midnight

Identifiers:
ISBN: 978-1-956292-03-9 (paperback)
ISBN: 978-1-956292-04-6 (hardcover)
ISBN: 978-1-956292-02-2 (e-book)

Subjects: Children's Fiction | Fiction-Action-Adventure
Face Your Fears | Never Give Up
Book Cover Design © 2021 by SUSU Entertainment LLC

Book Photography by SUSU Entertainment LLC

Table of Contents

Introduction

Do you find yourself saying "I can't" every time you are asked to do something? Children can often be selective in learning to try new things, usually saying "I can't." You probably haven't tried because you know if you say those two words someone will come running to your rescue. Have no fear, Captain Midnight is near! He can zap your fears away and give you the superpowers to be able to succeed and never give up.

Nothing is too hard for Captain Midnight, but he is sometimes challenged in space with the evil ways of the villain, Galatroid, but he is always determined to win the battle. Captain Midnight's motto is, "You were born strong and powerful! Face your fears and believe you can achieve if you try!"

Chapter 1

Be Open To
Try New Things

Mommy and Daddy were blessed with a baby boy named Miles. He was a very smart little boy with a big heart, but because he was the youngest, he was sometimes spoiled by his Mommy and sisters. Miles didn't always like to do things for himself. When he was asked to do anything he would say "I can't," and his sisters would run to his rescue. It wasn't a big problem to get help for Miles when he was a baby, but Mommy wanted him to be prepared when he started school to be able to do things on his own.

His big sisters always looked out for him, and although Mommy was happy they were very attentive to their baby brother, it made him very dependent on them. Miles's behavior had gotten out of hand, and being the baby brother he used it to his advantage. He didn't realize his sisters had gotten fed up because catering to him was exhausting.

One magical night, Mommy and Daddy prayed that Miles would put effort in helping himself more, and stop saying "I can't," and as they fell asleep they knew that their prayers would be answered for their baby boy.

Out from the sky, a bird, a Houston Rocket, a star shined bright and presented Captain Midnight! Captain Midnight was awakened by the fears of the world. He knew that with his superpowers he would be able to erase the words "I can't" to make it a better place for children all over the world. Captain Midnight zapped Miles with his laser beam as he was sleeping. He knew after his appearance Miles's life would never be the same.

As Miles woke up to the smell of breakfast, he couldn't believe how much energy he had, he was ready to conquer all of the things that he wasn't good at. Miles enjoyed spending time with his family, and going to the park was one of his favorite things to do. The family loved a day at the park, but for his sisters they couldn't always enjoy themselves because they were busy helping their baby brother get on and off the playground equipment.

Usually he would play it safe by getting on all the equipment that he was familiar with. Miles was fearful that if he tried something different, he would fall and hurt himself. He was a very tough little boy, but he was scared of trying to tackle new things.

Look, Miles faced his fears.

Mommy and Daddy talked to Miles about conquering his fears. They believed if they discussed how important it was to learn new things and never give up, he wouldn't be afraid. As his sisters were packing the picnic basket with a few of their favorite goodies like, turkey and cheese sandwiches, chips, fruit and garden salads, and chocolate chip cookies, Miles was anxiously waiting to go to the park, asking his parents every 5 minutes, "When are we leaving?"

They had finally arrived to the park, and Miles quickly disappeared. The girls assisted Mommy with setting up the picnic table. Daddy loved flying his kites, he had all sorts of large colorful kites such as, diamond kites, delta kites and box kites. Growing up in Louisiana this was one of his favorite things to do.

Miles and his Daddy also enjoyed playing basketball and football together. Miles would always enjoy assisting Daddy with putting the kites together, but this time, he was nowhere to be found. As the girls headed to the playground there was Miles on the monkey bars, tire swing, fireman's pole, corkscrew climber, and chin-up bar, it was all the playground equipment he was afraid to get on. He even enjoyed his favorite thing to do, jumping on the trampoline.

Captain Midnight had saved the day! Mommy and Daddy were so happy that Miles had faced his playground fears. It was the best day ever as they enjoyed a wonderful picnic and play day at the park.

Are you open to try new things?

Chapter 2

You Are What You Eat

"Sweets and Tings"

Tyra loved to bake sweet treats with her Mom. Her parents owned a family bakery called Sweets and Tings, and would make cupcakes, cookies, cakes, pastries and pies. Her Mom started baking as a little girl growing up in Kingston, Jamaica and introduced Tyra to her love of baking at an early age. Tyra was so fascinated with her family's bakery that she didn't really enjoy eating foods that were good for her, like fruits and vegetables.

Her parents begged Tyra to eat healthier because they didn't want her to get sick from not eating nutritious foods. They wanted her to eat fruits like apples, oranges, blueberries, strawberries, grapefruits and bananas, a very good source of vitamin A and vitamin C. Vegetables like green beans, carrots, okra, spinach, peas, broccoli, and sweet potatoes give you the vitamins and minerals needed to digest food and allow you to have a lot of energy.

Tyra's Mom explained to her if she tried a little she would be eating super foods, which will make her tummy smile. Tyra yelled, "I can't! I can't!" as she would gag at the thought of eating healthy. Her Mom told her she wouldn't be able to help her in the bakery if she didn't start eating her fruits and vegetables. Tyra began to cry because she loved helping her Mom bake cakes for weddings, graduations, anniversaries, baby showers and birthday parties.

M
KABOOM!

Her parents knew that her feelings were hurt, but needed to find a way to make Tyra enjoy eating healthier. Captain Midnight heard her cry and was anxious to put a smile back on Tyra's face again. During the night, Captain Midnight appeared but had to fight off the villain Galatroid, who wanted to keep the children fearful and full of the words "I can't."

Captain Midnight knew that Tyra needed his help but he had to hurry because midnight was approaching and he had to stop Galatroid from trying to take his superpowers away. Galatroid was a villain that lived in space and didn't like to see Captain Midnight helping children face their fears. Galatroid liked the world to be afraid because he liked sadness.

As Captain Midnight flew to help Tyra, Galatroid tried to spray him with his poisonous venom which would put Captain Midnight to sleep, not allowing him to make it in time to help Tyra. Galatroid had many tricks he used with his boomerangs to make Captain Midnight loose his balance and eventually fall, but because Captain Midnight was a human rocket, he was very quick as he used his shield to dodge Galatroid.

It was a game of tug of war in the sky, but suddenly Captain Midnight used his mighty fist, shield and powerful net and KAPOW! BOOM! ZAP! WHAM! He punched Galatroid so hard, he began seeing stars! Captain Midnight immediately sprayed his powerful net around Galatroid to keep him away from Tyra and her family.

Captain Midnight was happy that Galatroid was knocked out and tied up in space. He hurried to save Tyra from her unhealthy eating habits, and as she slept like a little princess, he zapped her with his laser beam. The next day Tyra asked her Mom if she could try some spinach, but it was too early because she was preparing breakfast.

Tyra and her Mom started putting together ingredients from the refrigerator and surprisingly the family enjoyed a tasty cheddar bacon, spinach and egg breakfast casserole! Captain Midnight rescued Tyra from her fears of eating healthy foods, and the family was so happy to have Tyra back helping in the family bakery again.

What are your favorite fruits and vegetables?

Chapter 3

Use Your Special Talents

Ashton was a very talented little boy. He enjoyed playing games with his dog Jasper and loved to draw but didn't feel his artworks were as good as some of his classmates. Ashton didn't have much excitement in life anymore after his Mom had passed away.

He was raised by his Dad, and although they had a great relationship, he was often saddened by his Mom's absence. Ashton had several of his drawings and paintings stuffed away in his closet. His Dad noticed his son's talent at an early age, and asked him to enter them in the school's art contest.

Ashton didn't believe in himself, usually saying the words "I can't," because he was scared he would be laughed at or teased for the things he would draw. Many days had gone by and the school's art contest was getting closer and closer. His Dad reminisced about how he was a little boy, growing up in the United Kingdom, having a dream of being an artist but because he was afraid and didn't have anyone to push him toward his dreams, he ignored them.

Dad prayed for his son to believe in himself, because he knew if he didn't, he would not be the best he could be. Captain Midnight heard the conversation between Ashton and his Dad. He knew his superpowers were needed because the contest was in five days.

Captain Midnight was truly busy that night, because he had to reach every child by midnight or his superpowers wouldn't work. After Ashton enjoyed a bedtime story from his Dad, he laid in bed dreaming of winning his school's art contest. He fell asleep when Captain Midnight appeared, zapping the laser beam on Ashton.

On his way back to space Captain Midnight had to fight off Galatroid. He had to fly all over the galaxy to dodge Galatroid's poisonous venom and his new weapon, a crossbow. Captain Midnight's laser beam was used to distract Galatroid from seeing clearly and save the children from their fears. Although he was distracted, Captain Midnight was happy he had saved Ashton in time for the contest.

SCHOOL
1

The next morning there was something different about Ashton, he was happy and had so much confidence while gathering his most recent drawings. He asked his Dad to stop by the store on their way to school to buy him a new art case for his drawings. His Dad was thrilled at Ashton's new attitude. Ashton entered the contest and surprisingly he won 1st place! He was happy to receive a beautiful golden trophy and was asked by his art teacher to be a student helper for the month.

Ashton didn't understand that even though he thought his drawings were nothing, the judges were impressed with his abstract artworks complete with beautiful shapes and colors. Captain Midnight gleamed with excitement that Ashton never said "I can't" again, and his new phrase became "I can do anything!"

What are your hobbies?

Chapter 4

The Greatest Love Of All

Danielle and Donovan were 12-year-old biracial twins born in Cleveland, Ohio to a young mother who wasn't ready to raise a child, especially not twins. They were put in foster care as newborns and always prayed to be adopted by a wonderful and loving family. Danielle was born first and was like a mother to Donovan, always making sure he was eating, had clean clothes and was never mistreated. When they thought they were getting close to being adopted, something would happen and it never worked out, leaving them to stay another year at the foster home. They felt sad seeing so many others younger than them being adopted. They often wondered why no one wanted two adorable and helpful 12-year-olds.

Danielle would bring her dolls along everywhere she would go to show off her sewing skills. She taught herself how to sew doll clothes from scraps of cloth that the staff left behind and would put in the trash. Donovan loved to play football, so he would carry his football tucked under his arms to show his catching and throwing skills. Some of the other kids would laugh, telling them that no one wanted them because they were too old, because babies were the top picks for adoptions. This would hurt Donovan's feelings and he would cry because he felt like no one loved him. The constant rejections they faced caused Donovan to shut down and the things he enjoyed most in life, like reading, playing football and video games he stopped doing.

Danielle was very outgoing, strong-willed, and determined to be adopted. She told Donovan not to worry because things would change very soon. She knew God would bless them with a loving and caring family. Donovan became very sad, and not being adopted made him not want to participate in school activities. He ate very little, became less talkative, and surprisingly, he stopped playing his favorite sport, football. Anytime Donovan was asked to do anything, he replied by saying "I can't." Donovan wasn't happy with his life, because he wanted a family of his own. Once a month they had Adoption Day and Donovan feared going because he knew what the outcome would be.

BOOM!
M

Danielle prayed and asked for help in finding a family that loved 12-year-olds. Donovan's favorite holiday was Christmas and when the Christmas wish list was passed to him to complete, he filled it out and stated "A LOVING FAMILY" in big, bold letters. Donovan's entire life was filled with "I can't," he was afraid of being happy because he knew that sadness would soon follow. Captain Midnight had been listening to Danielle and Donovan's plea to find a family. He knew that Donovan's change of behavior was because he felt unloved and he became fearful by not doing the things that brought him joy.

Captain Midnight had a big job to do that night, he had to zap Donovan back to realizing that in time, he would be adopted by the perfect family, but he couldn't live in fear and not enjoy his life as it is now. He also had to zap a family that had lost their children in a car accident to not be fearful to love again. This caused for double duty of zapping fears away. Captain Midnight helps children face their fears but was determined to make his superpowers work on the parents who grieved children too. Sometimes in life, when trouble is at its worst, and you don't know which way to turn, a blessing is right around the corner.

Captain Midnight had double trouble with Galatroid that night, constantly having to use his super weapons to fight him away. Galatroid knew that Captain Midnight had a lot of saving to do, so he tried very hard to distract him until after midnight, when his superpowers wouldn't work. Galatroid threw his boomerang and hit Captain Midnight, knocking him in the head. Captain Midnight laid very still until Galatroid was out of sight, he got up feeling very dizzy and flew quickly to Donovan and zapped him with his laser beam. He scurried to the family that had recently lost their children in hopes that they would find it in their heart to love again. The next day, only one day before Christmas, Donovan's wish was granted!

A couple came to Adoption Day looking for 12-year-old twins to provide a loving and happy home to. The couple had recently lost their 12-year-old twins, a girl and a boy in a car accident. They were hit by a teenager that was texting while driving. It was very sad because they were coming home from cheerleading and football practice. The parents started a non-profit organization to raise awareness and help reach everyone to stop texting while driving.

Danielle and Donovan were overjoyed when they found out that the couple wanted to raise them as their own, and the greatest of all, the Mom was a fashion designer, owning her own fashion boutique and the Dad was a high school football coach. Captain Midnight was so happy he was able to put them together to face their fears of not being loved, to loving again with so much in common.

What do you love about your family?

____

____

____

____

____

____

____

Chapter 5

Practice Makes Perfect

Yes son, you can learn it.

Chung was a very smart little boy that had recently moved to the United States with his parents from China. He was more advanced than his peers in Kindergarten, already able to multiply and divide. He enjoyed school, and although he was confused of some words in the English language, he continued to study and use his neighbors to help him with his sight words. Chung was an A+ student, but was very shy. He didn't like when the teacher called on him to answer questions in class, although he knew the answers, he didn't like the attention. Chung had one thing that he couldn't quite grasp, and that was tying his shoes. Mom and Dad would work with him for hours, but there was no luck. Chung got really frustrated and quit trying.

Dad explained to Chung step by step but he didn't understand how to make the bunny rabbit ears. Chung hollered, "I can't! I can't!" A few of Chung's classmates would take turns helping him tie his shoes. One day the worst thing happened, the class bully Baxter volunteered to help Chung tie his shoes, but when Chung went to run during recess, he didn't realize that Baxter had tied both of his shoes together, making him fall on his face in the dirt. Chung was embarrassed and upset because everyone turned to him pointing and laughing.

Yes, I did it

When he got home, he told his parents what had happened and never wanted to go back to school again. Mom and Dad knew that they needed help, because their son was happy to learn, but because of the embarrassing fall, things would never be the same. Captain Midnight heard Chung's cry and his parent's plea for help for their son. As Dad prayed and tucked Chung in bed, he saw that all of his son's shoes were piled high in the trash can, he was truly hurt. Dad wiped his son's tears, and assured Chung that one day, he would be tying his shoes with no problem.

Captain Midnight appeared that night with his laser beam and zapped it over Chung. This was an easy night for Captain Midnight because Galatroid the villain was nowhere in sight. Dad was waiting for Chung as he got off the bus with a pair of his favorite sneakers. Without hesitation, Chung started to tie his own shoes! He couldn't believe it! Chung was so excited he couldn't wait to show off his skills to his classmates.

Mom and Dad were so impressed they shouted it out to the neighbors! They all rejoiced that Chung had conquered his fears and learned how to tie his shoes. Chung was so happy that he started asking to tie everyone's shoes. Chung learned from Captain Midnight that if at first you don't succeed, try again and again.

Do you have any goals you are working on?

Chapter 6

Face Your Fears

Isabella was very cute and had a smile that would brighten up an entire room. What her friends didn't know was that she was afraid of bugs. She loved to play outside with her friends, but because of her fear of bugs, she would only watch her friends from her bedroom window. Her fear came from being bitten by a mosquito that caused her to swell really badly.

The next day, her neighbor chased her with a beetle bug and threw it on her, leaving Isabella to be fearful of the outdoors. Isabella's parents would often persuade her to go outside and enjoy her friends, but she knew something outside would eventually frighten her. She would often beg her parents to write her teachers a note to skip P.E. and recess, which was a great time for kids to play with their friends and get the daily exercise needed.

Isabella wanted to overcome her fear and stop using words like "I can't" because it was truly stopping her from having fun with her friends. She loved flowers and would often see her favorite flowers being eaten by the bugs, which caused her to be even more afraid of going outside. Her Mom would put bug repellent spray on her to keep the bugs away, but nothing seemed to help her overcome her fear of the outdoors. Her parents knew something had to change.

Captain Midnight wanted Isabella to have an enjoyable life and decided to help her. As Captain Midnight soared towards the house he was approached by the villain Galatroid who liked to see the world full of fear and liked using words like "I can't." Captain Midnight didn't like violence but he had to protect the world. He only had a few minutes before it would be too late to save Isabella before midnight.

Captain Midnight released his weapons, a laser beam, shield, fist, and his handy net, and was ready for battle. His superpowers were activated. WHAM! KABOOM! ZAP! BOING! SPLAT! WHACK! Captain Midnight punched Galatroid sending him flying into space. Oh, no! Captain Midnight had only 5 seconds to save Isabella. He flew as fast as he could to make it in time. He arrived at her house and 5, 4, 3, 2, 1, she was zapped by the laser beam!

Isabella's parents surprised her with a brand new bike to overcome her fear of the outdoors. Isabella washed her face, brushed her teeth, got dressed, said her grace, ate her breakfast, and played outside with her friends all day, later riding her new bike into the sunset. Thanks to Captain Midnight, she was the happiest girl alive.

What fears do you want to overcome?

____

____

____

____

____

____

____

____

Chapter 7

Reading Is Fun

United States
Ghana
Sri Lanka
World Map

Kumasi moved to the United States with his parents and siblings from Ghana. He was an active 10-year-old who loved to read and explore. As a 4th grader, he was very smart in school in Ghana but after moving, he lacked interest in reading books because of the native American language, which caused him to experience trouble with pronunciation of words, spelling, and reading comprehension. Kumasi was liked by most of his classmates, it wasn't hard for him to gain many friends at school.

Nirved was Kumasi's best friend and his parents were from India, but after he was born they moved to the United States. Kumasi and Nirved lived in the same neighborhood and rode the bus together. Everyone loved to hear Kumasi tell stories of fun things to do in Ghana, such as, shop at the market, sightsee at the museums, visit the wildlife sanctuary, botanical gardens, and shop at the adinkra cloth village, known for its symbols and proverbial wisdom. Many admired his accent, but some poked fun at him because of the difficulties he had with understanding some of the English language.

Although Kumasi and his family understood English, Akan is their first spoken language. Kumasi is embarrassed when his teacher asked him to read out loud in front of the class. She takes turns with each student, and now it is Kumasi's turn. He begins to get so nervous that he starts to stutter and quickly request a restroom break.

Kumasi thinks of every excuse not to read that day. "My stomach hurts," he explains to the teacher. "The writing in the book is too small, I can't read it," says Kumasi. "May I switch reading days?" He asked. He starts to truly hate what he loved in Ghana, school.

M
M

Kumasi was born into a family of readers because his Mom is a librarian, his Dad is a professor at the local University and his siblings always seem to request books for their birthdays and holiday gifts. Nirved understood what Kumasi was going through because his older siblings had to adjust to the native English language because they were born in Sri Lanka.

Relocating is very hard, especially when it is to a new country. It is very important to explore and research the culture and environment before moving. You will definitely have to adjust to the native language, gain new friends, and accept that sometimes you may get homesick. Kumasi's fear of reading became worse.

Mom and Dad knew something had to be done because they were concerned that their son's fear of reading in English would start to affect his grades. Everyday Kumasi started saying a new phrase, "I can't read these books." It had gotten so bad that reading a book felt like a punishment to Kumasi instead of enjoyment like before.

Just in the nick of time, Captain Midnight heard Kumasi's parents praying to help their son get his love of reading back, but it was hard for Captain Midnight to zap him that night because Galatroid was waiting close by. Captain Midnight tried to hustle and bustle to Kumasi's home before midnight but not without a fight with Galatroid. BOOM! WHACK! KAPOW!

LIBRARY
BIOGRAFI

The two fought tirelessly in the sky, because unlike Captain Midnight, Galatroid loved for children to live in fear. Captain Midnight was so happy that he had won the fight with Galatroid and was able to zap Kumasi with his laser beam. The next day, Kumasi woke up feeling refreshed and renewed ready to conquer his fear of reading out loud in his class.

When Mrs. Lacey asked for a volunteer to read the book of the day, Kumasi quickly raised his hands. Kumasi read to his class, only making a few mistakes. His confidence and positive attitude had him feeling truly unstoppable. Kumasi practiced reading every day and learned new vocabulary words.

His understanding and comprehension skills improved, and being a better reader helped him complete his assignments on time. He even noticed when he gained more confidence in reading, his writing started to improve as well. Kumasi started encouraging everyone to read every day to increase their vocabulary, build fluency and comprehension. He was so happy that reading books brought him joy again.

What are your favorite books to read?

Dedication

We dedicate this book to our smart, loving, active, soft-spoken, and gentle-hearted 10-year-old son Nalin. If you have ever had any fears, always saying "I can't," this book is for you. You will learn through prayer, strength, family support, and Captain Midnight's laser beam, that if you work hard, and believe in yourself, you can do anything you want to do to accomplish your goals. You are super smart, super loved, and we are super proud of you. Learn to try new things, and if at first you don't succeed, try again and again. We all live with a superhero in our hearts. Recharge your superpowers!

Love,

Mommy & Daddy

About the Author

LaWanda Lewis Burrell is a native of Greenville, Alabama but has lived in the Houston, Texas area for over 20 years. She is a wife and mother of three beautiful children. Mrs. Burrell is the Co-Founder of SUSU Entertainment LLC, a book writing, audiobook narrating, and publishing company with her husband, Founder DeMorris Burrell, Jr.

Mrs. Burrell is also the author of Stand Up, Speak Up, Because Your Time's Up, an inspirational journey of her life where she had to use her voice to stand up and speak up for her beliefs. She is a former HR professional and educator where she has had a love for literature and working with children. Through her trials of life, she discovered her passion of writing which often mimics her personality and inspires you to live a happy and fearless life of possibilities.

About the Co-Author

Nalin Chase Burrell is a shy, kind, competitive and cool, pizza-loving 10- year-old and is the baby of the family. He is a native of Houston, Texas and enjoys many hobbies like, reading comics, playing football and basketball, board games with the family, baking sweets and treats, swimming, traveling, photography, playing video games with his sisters, and co-writing his first book.

Nalin didn't always enjoy reading as he struggled in articulation and expressive language skills. What helped his progression was to read a book every night for 20 minutes. Through his hard work, support from his parents and teachers, and self-confidence, he continues to strive in excellence to be a lifelong learner and better reader!

www.ingramcontent.com/pod-product-compliance
Lightning Source LLC
Chambersburg PA
CBHW040727010826
48981CB00031B/304